/98
OKS
198

1628
TWO CHIMNEYS

Mary Z. Holmes
Illustrated by Geri Strigenz

STONE
BANK
BOOKS

RAINTREE
STECK-VAUGHN
LIBRARY
Austin, Texas

* For Mother *

This text and art were reviewed for accuracy by Nancy Egloff and Brenda Rosseau, Staff Historians, Jamestown Settlement, Williamsburg, VA.

Designed by Geri Strigenz

Published by Raintree/Steck-Vaughn Library
P.O. Box 26015, Austin, TX 78755

Library of Congress Cataloging-in-Publication Data
Holmes, Mary Z.
    Two chimneys / Mary Z. Holmes ; illustrated by Geri Strigenz.
        p. cm. — (History's children)
    "A Stone Bank Book."
    Summary: Having lived in Virginia for six years since 1622, Katherine does not want to leave her family's tobacco plantation after learning of her betrothment to an English heir.
    ISBN 0-8114-3506-7. — ISBN 0-8114-6431-8 (pbk.)
    1. Jamestown (Va.)—History—Juvenile fiction. 2. Virginia—History—Colonial period, ca. 1600-1775—Juvenile fiction. [1. Jamestown (Va.)—History—Fiction. 2. Virginia—History—Colonial period, ca. 1600-1775—Fiction.] I. Strigenz, Geri K., ill. II. Title. III. Series: Holmes, Mary Z. History's children.
PZ7.H7375Tw 1992   91-35817
[Fic]—dc20   CIP AC

Printed in the United States of America
1 2 3 4 5 6 7 8 9 WZ 96 95 94 93 92

1628

*T*his story takes place along the James River, in what is now the state of Virginia. In 1628, people from England are living here. For twenty-one years, they have struggled to keep their small settlement going.

The people in Virginia are a long way from their original home in England across the Atlantic Ocean. They work hard to make a new life for themselves. There is danger from Indian attacks and sickness. Life has been hard, and many people have died.

I
THE PLANTATION

I came to Virginia with my family in the summer of 1622. I was seven years old.

There's little that I remember about coming here. We were on the ocean for what seemed to be forever. Mother wouldn't let us from her sight. We stayed in the cramped space within the ship's hold or huddled next to her on the windy deck above. She wouldn't let us run around. And that's what I wanted to do most of all.

My sister, Rosemund, was eleven years old. She was bossy and acted just like Mother in watching over me. Her hair was a lovely strawberry blond. Even at her young age, she was a perfect little lady.

I wasn't a perfect little lady. Grandmother told me that I was a wild thing. She teased me and said that my hair was too red for a lady. I remember her. She stayed in England.

Little Henry, my younger brother, was only two years old. He cried most of the way to Virginia. The rising and falling of the ship gave him an upset stomach. When he was feeling better, Henry didn't want to be still, so he cried then too. It was my job to play games with him and make him laugh. If I got too wild with him, Mother would box my ears. Then I would cry, and that made Henry cry all over again. It was a terrible, long journey.

My older brother, Robert, didn't come with us. He stayed in England for his education. The plan was to have him join us when he turned eighteen. He was only twelve then, but he seemed very grown-up to me. I remember him standing on the dock waving good-bye to us when we sailed from England. I missed Robert. Mother did too. She talked about him often.

Father had paid the cost of the journey for twelve other people, in addition to our family. These people were to be our servants until this money was repaid. They would belong to us for seven years and then be free. The servants would help us start a tobacco plantation on the Virginia land belonging to Father. Some of them were sick on the ship, and Father watched over them.

My father was an English gentleman. His family owned an estate in England. When his father died, all the land was given to Father's older brother. Since Father didn't have a home anymore, he decided to bring us to Virginia. Here we would become rich growing tobacco. That was his dream.

The ship finally arrived at the Virginia shore and sailed up the James River to Jamestown. I remember being thrilled to have my feet on land again. Henry and I ran along the streets of the little town. Rosemund ran after and scolded us for misbehaving. We were too young to notice the unhappy people of Jamestown.

We arrived during a starving time. Earlier that spring, the Indians had attacked the plantations on the James River and killed many of the settlers. The survivors fled from their homes to safety at Jamestown. This was before they could plant their crops. Now, in the summer, there was little food.

Father found us a place with a Jamestown family. We crowded together in the little cottage, all of us sleeping in a single room. The summer was hot and sticky. Henry and I complained about wearing our heavy clothes, and Mother's temper was short. I remember feeling itchy from the hot clothes. Where my skin showed, I was covered with mosquito bites.

Then the sickness struck, and people began to die. When people died in the house where we were staying, Father said that we were moving away from Jamestown, even if the Indians were dangerous. So our family, the servants, the livestock that had come with us on the ship, and our supplies were sailed farther upriver to our land. We called it Eastwood's Plantation. That's my father's name, William Eastwood.

At first, it was a great adventure. We lived in tents. The servants cut down trees to clear some land. Then they put up the palisade — a high fence with watchtowers that would protect us from the Indians. Inside the palisade, work began on the house for our family. I wanted to help too, but Mother said that young ladies didn't do that kind of work. So Henry and I ran free and got into no end of trouble.

But we couldn't outrun the sickness. Henry died first. He tired early one day and lay down to rest in the tent. He had a high fever. The next day he was dead. His grave was the first one that was dug. Before I could get through a whole day without weeping, Rosemund sickened and died. In the first year we were at the plantation, over half our servants died too. I don't like to think about it.

The next few years aren't clear in my memory. I felt alone without my little brother and big sister. And I missed my brother in England. I remember that.

The servants worked hard to develop the plantation. Our two-room cottage was completed, and we moved in. I slept in a loft under the roof of the cottage. Outside the palisade, we built a house for the women servants and a barn where the men servants stayed. Land was cleared for tobacco, food crops, and the orchards. Our wharf was built at the river's edge. When they weren't working in the tobacco fields, the men built a shed, a milkhouse where cheese and butter would be made, and the warehouse where the tobacco would be cured and stored.

The burial ground grew too. Each year, Father sent for new servants from England. Each year, about half the new servants died. Virginia was an unhealthy place for newcomers.

We've been here at Eastwood's Plantation for six years now. Virginia is home to me. This is where I belong. It is 1628, and I'm thirteen years old. I still have hair that's too red for a lady. Mother says I'm a wild thing. She sounds just like Grandmother.

* * *

"Katherine, stand still," Mother commanded. I was trying on a gown that had belonged to Rosemund. I couldn't help but wiggle and pull at the tight sleeves. Mother knelt in front of the trunk that held her greatest treasures.

"This gown doesn't fit me," I said. "It's too small."

Mother frowned and motioned me to turn around. "Anne, what do you think?"

"Too tight," Anne said. "Too short." She was the seamstress who sewed, mended, and remade old clothes for us.

"Oh, bother," Mother said as she dug through the things in the trunk. She pushed aside packets of needles, thread, lace, and old clothes. "Katherine, you're so in-between. You're too big for Rosemund's old clothes, God bless her. And you're too small to wear anything of mine."

I thought about Rosemund, who had died years ago. She had looked so pretty in this gown. What would she say if she could see how I dressed now? I wore the same clothes as the servants, except when a special occasion arose. Then Mother would fuss and try to find something else — something more ladylike.

Anne coughed and said, "Mistress, maybe I could cut the skirt. I'll use it to make a jacket for Miss Katherine. She can wear it over her everyday gown."

"It will have to do." Mother closed the trunk with a thump and looked at me. "Katherine, take that gown off and let Anne get to work on it."

I quickly obeyed. That was the best thing to do when Mother was in this mood. I knew what had her in a tizzy. My brother Robert was arriving from England within a few weeks. He was a young gentleman now, and Mother wanted everything to be in order for him. I was one of her problems. Mother was trying to turn me into a lady overnight.

As I put on my everyday gown, she looked me over closely. "What are we going to do with your hair?" she asked. "And where are your shoes?"

"Here they are," I said, holding up my shoes. They pinched my feet, but I wasn't about to say anything. I didn't have any other shoes. Mother sighed and pushed me out the door.

Freedom. I ran across the yard and out of the palisade. I bent over to hide my shoes in the long grass. They really did hurt my feet. For the past few weeks, I'd been leaving the shoes here and going barefoot. Mother didn't know.

I walked over to the women's house and peeked in the doorway. It had only one room, so I could see at a glance that the women servants weren't there. Then I heard shouting behind me. I turned and saw that it was the servant Jane.

"What is it?" I called.

"Hog in the vegetable garden," Jane yelled back as she ran past me. Oh, good, I thought, something exciting. And off I went.

The hog was running through the cabbages and onions with Jane after it. I ran around to the other side of the garden, hoping to get there first and head off the hog. But it was too fast. It turned around sharply and headed through the carrots.

"Your head will be on the chopping block," I screamed, "if you don't get out of this garden." Our hogs ran free in the woods, and sometimes they got into the gardens. We didn't have to catch this hog. We just had to chase it back to the woods. The best thing to do was to scare it away.

"Off with your head," Jane yelled and waved her apron at the hog. I flapped my arms in the air and ran screaming at it.

"Katherine!" Someone called. Turning to look, I tripped over a cabbage and fell flat to the ground. It was my father who had called. I got up and brushed the dirt off my clothes. Tucking my hair back into my cap, I walked over to him.

"I know, Father," I said. "I'm a wild thing. I'm out of control. And whatever are we going to do about me?"

Father winked at me. "Well, Katherine, at least we know you're not a lady yet," he said. "Now get your shoes from your hiding place. We'd better have another talk with your mother."

He had known about the shoes all along. Now mother would find out.

II
JAMESTOWN

Mother's burst of temper wasn't as bad as I expected. Maybe it was because Robert was arriving soon. Her mind was more on him than on me. But she kept me at her side for the next several days as a lesson.

I would learn how to be a lady from her. That's what she said. She would teach me. In England, a lady didn't actually do any of the work. A lady decided what to do and directed the women servants to do it, she told me. Here in Virginia, before we had enough servants, Mother had worked hard too. But now was the time to begin acting like ladies, she said.

Father, of course, was in charge of the men. All the men on our plantation worked in the tobacco fields — clearing land, planting, weeding, worming, harvesting, and then curing. It kept them busy most of the year. When the year's crop was in the warehouse, then they turned their attention to building and fencing.

It was up to the lady of the house to see that the family and servants were fed. When we first came here, there was little food. In the early years on Eastwood's Plantation, Indian corn and wild game kept us alive. But with Mother in charge, we soon had gardens and orchards planted. We grew carrots, pumpkins, cabbages, peas, onions, potatoes, turnips, parsnips, apples, and pears. And there were fields of wheat, barley, and corn.

The women servants grew the food and tended the livestock. Our cattle, goats, and hogs had grown in number over the years. We had many chickens and ducks in the yard behind the women's house. These animals were important for food. Sometimes Mother asked Father to have a hunt. Then we'd have deer meat and, in the right season, wild ducks and other birds. The men fished too, and brought back clams and oysters as a special treat.

Mother decided what would be planted and where. She decided when animals would be butchered. She decided what we would eat. It was a lady's duty, she said, and I must learn it. The servants would do the actual work.

I was glad Mother didn't know that I did servant work whenever I could get away with it. I loved to plant and harvest, feed the chickens, and collect the eggs. Chasing hogs was one of my favorite jobs. I even helped in the tobacco fields when Father was away. I knew as much about tobacco as some of the men did. They kept my work a secret from my parents. I think it amused them.

The lady of the house also saw that everyone had clothes to wear. It was a big problem for Mother this summer. We didn't have enough shoes. Some of the men's clothes looked like rags. Robert was bringing new shoes and cloth with him from England. We couldn't wait for him to come.

I stood at Mother's side early one morning as she talked with Anne about mending and with Jane about weeding the gardens. Sarah cooked and worked in the milkhouse. Mother talked to her about making cheese. I was itching to get away and see what was happening in the tobacco fields.

I saw someone tie up a boat at the wharf and said, "Mother, someone is here. Look." I pointed as a man began to run toward us from the river.

"Mistress," he shouted. "The ship's at Jamestown."

"Oh, goodness." Mother put her hand to her throat. "He must mean Robert's ship." Then she called, "Be a good man and tell Mr. Eastwood for us. He's in the west field."

The man waved his arm and ran off to look for Father.

With her eyes sparkling, Mother gave directions. "Sarah, prepare for a feast. Chickens, ducks, hams, bread and honey, cheese, apple cider," she said excitedly. "Jane, see which vegetables are ready. Anne, make sure there's bedding for the new servants Robert is bringing. And have Thomas get his fiddle out. We'll have dancing tonight."

I was jumping up and down. Robert's ship was in.

Mother put her hand on my head to steady me. "Oh dear," she said as she looked me over. "Is Katherine's jacket ready, Anne?"

"Yes, ma'am."

"Then see that she's dressed. Get out my best gown and Mr. Eastwood's good things." She clapped her hands. "Let's get busy. We're going to Jamestown to welcome Robert."

Within the hour, we were ready to leave. Father, Mother, and I got in the boat. The man who had come to get us hoisted the sails, and we began to move down the river. He would take us to Jamestown. Robert's ship would bring us back. Riding in an oceangoing ship would be only part of the day's excitement. Best of all, I'd see Robert again.

The morning was sunny and hot, but cooler on the water. We floated pleasantly downriver. I stood at the front of the boat, listening to my parents talk.

"William," Mother was saying to Father. "What will Robert be like? He was so young when we left."

Father patted her hand. "I'm sure he's a fine young gentleman now, Elizabeth. He's been well educated."

"My little boy," Mother sighed.

"Not so little anymore, my dear."

"Sometimes I feel as if I know him from his letters," Mother said as she watched the riverbank float by. "We've exchanged so many letters over the years. Even Katherine has written to him."

Father smiled. He was thinking of my letters with the big spots of ink all over them. Mother had taught me how to read and write, but I wasn't very good.

"After six years, how can we really know him?" Mother asked.

"Don't worry," Father said. "He's still our Robert."

I turned to where they were sitting and said, "Think of all the wonderful things Robert is bringing, Mother. He may even have shoes that fit me."

We all laughed at that. I shifted from foot to foot, suddenly reminded of the tight shoes I was wearing. It would be a blessing to have new ones.

We drifted past another plantation and could see small boats in the water. Men were fishing under the hot sun.

Father took off his hat and wiped his forehead. "Did I happen to mention the surprise Robert is bringing?"

He had our full attention. We waited for him to go on. Father could be a tease. Finally, Mother urged him to tell us, but he wouldn't.

"No, no. It wouldn't be fair to spoil a surprise," he said.

Mother and I pretended to be angry with him for a while. I wasn't really angry, but it did bother me when he teased us. Mother's mood became happier. She stopped worrying about Robert. I knew she was wondering about the surprise.

Jamestown finally came into view. As we sailed closer, I could see three big sailing ships at the wharves. When we pulled in, I was out of the boat before Mother had a chance to stop me.

There was a bustle of activity. The children of Jamestown ran back and forth. Pale, shaky passengers stood in small groups, trying to get the feel of solid ground again. Other Virginia planters like my father moved from group to group. They were looking for family or servants just arrived from England. The crew of one ship was lowering supplies with ropes and pulleys. Men shouted at people to move out of the way.

I pushed through the crowd, looking for Robert. I bumped into a tobacco merchant who was talking business. "Move aside, girl," he said with a nasty look.

I looked among the groups of passengers. Some of them were sitting on the ground, feeling weak from the heat. They were new servants, not gentlemen. Where was Robert? I realized I no longer knew what he looked like.

Then Father called me. I turned and saw him standing with two young gentlemen. One of them was giving Mother a big hug. It had to be my brother. He looked over at me as Father pointed me out. He was handsome and dressed in splendid clothes. His hair was long. He carried a walking stick. I thought he was wonderful.

"Is that my Kat?" Robert shouted.

"Robert?" I called and ran to him.

He picked me up and twirled me around. I slipped my arms around his neck and hung on, laughing.

Then he put me down and stood back to have a look. "My little sister. I can't believe it," he said. "Grown even wilder. I say, Mother, Kat looks like a servant girl."

Mother frowned and looked away. I blinked back tears. How dare he say that I looked like a servant!

"Come, Kat," Robert said, "and meet my good friend, Edward Hollyman. He's going to stay at the plantation with us."

I looked at the young gentleman with Robert. I think I greeted him properly, but I was too upset by what Robert had said about me to care. I don't remember what Edward Hollyman said to me in return. All I saw was a kind look in his bright blue eyes. He has nicer eyes than Robert, I thought angrily.

I stood to the side as Father talked to the ship's captain. After Jamestown's supplies were unloaded from the ship, it would take us home. Robert and Mother huddled close together, and I could hear them talking and laughing. Edward Hollyman watched the activity on the shore. He seemed interested in everything that was going on.

Finally, we were aboard the sailing ship on our way to the plantation. My feet hurt. I was very unhappy.

"Well, Kat," Robert said. "Come stand by me and tell me all about Virginia." He put his arm around my shoulder. "I've missed you, my pretty sister."

"I missed you too, Robert," I said honestly. I felt much better. Being on a ship next to my brother was the best thing in the world.

III
SURPRISES FROM ENGLAND

"This is our house?" Robert asked as we stood before our cottage. "I had no idea you lived as poorly as this."

When we had gotten off the ship at the plantation wharf late that day, Father said we would unload tomorrow. This night was special. It was a night for food and dancing. The servants Robert had brought were greeted and shown where they'd live. The ship's crew sat at the wharf and relaxed. Father led Robert and Edward Hollyman to the palisade. That's when Robert first saw the cottage.

Robert looked around at our family. "It's like a peasant hut, isn't it?" he asked.

Father looked disappointed with Robert. Mother was at a loss for words. I was stunned.

Edward cleared his throat and said, "How wonderful it is. Your people built the cottage themselves and all the other buildings? How much you've done."

"Oh, of course," Robert said with some embarassment. "I'm sorry, Father. It's quite a victory to have built all of this. Do forgive me."

The uneasy moment passed. I was comforted to see Sarah preparing food for the feast. An outside fire was going, and a table was heavy with things to eat and drink.

"Katherine, call everyone into the palisade," Mother said to me. "It's time to eat."

I forgot about being a lady and ran as fast as I could to the women's house. Jane introduced me to Alice and Mercey, the two new girls. Both of them were young, about my age. Alice looked sad. Mercey was very shy.

"I'm so happy that you got here safely," I said to them. "What you need is a good meal and a long rest. Everything will look better tomorrow." Poor things, I thought. "Jane, take them up to the palisade. The feast is ready."

There were eight new men servants at the barn. One of them was lying on the dirt floor, already asleep. Thomas said not to wake him. Sleep was what he needed. I told the men to get up to the palisade for the feast and made sure that Thomas took his fiddle with him.

Everyone else was at the wharf. "Come join us," I called, and they came eagerly up the path.

The evening went well. After everyone had eaten as much as they could, Father raised his cup and said, "God save the king." Then we celebrated with songs and dancing. I took off my tight shoes and hoped Mother wouldn't see. Robert taught me the latest dances from England.

"You're quite a girl, Kat," Robert said as we danced.

"So are you," I said. "I mean, you're quite a gentleman, Robert. So manly." I laughed as we twirled around the fire to the fiddle's tune. "But why is your hair so long?"

Robert touched the dark hair that rested on his shoulders, "This is how King Charles wears his hair. It's the new style."

"I suppose we're hopelessly out of style in Virginia?"

"Well, Kat, bare feet are hardly in style in England," he said, pointing to my feet. "Not for ladies anyway."

"Oh, bother," I said. I sounded just like Mother. "We don't have any shoes that fit. I couldn't dance with tight shoes, could I?"

He lifted me high and set me down again. It was part of the dance. "We shall make a lady of you tomorrow. I've brought new shoes from England. So many shoes you won't know what to do with them all." I'd forgotten about the supplies on the ship waiting to be unloaded and about Father's surprise. I asked Robert what else was on the ship for us, but he wouldn't say.

"I promised Father not to say another word," he said. I could have shaken him.

As the hour grew late, the servants drifted off. One by one, the ship's crew returned to the wharf. I sat by the fire listening to Father and Robert talk about King Charles and the European war. It was too far away to interest me. I was thinking about the surprise.

"Miss Eastwood?" Edward Hollyman drew me from my thoughts. "May I?" He gestured to the log on which I was sitting.

"Yes, please sit down," I turned my attention to him. He had wonderful blue eyes and sandy hair. He was about eighteen, Robert's age, and wore plainer clothes than my brother. He was a gentleman, but not as splendid as Robert. "Who are you?" I asked.

Edward laughed. The question was too direct, I thought. I wanted to be proper with our guest, so I tried again. "What I mean to say is, tell me about yourself."

"I'm the son of a preacher," he said. "My family saw to it that I was educated. That's where I met your brother. At school. After school, I had no chances in England. My family didn't have money to set me up in a proper occupation, you see."

I nodded. He was talking to me seriously, as if I were older. He made me feel important.

"Robert suggested I come to Virginia and try to make my fortune in tobacco," Edward continued. "Your father has agreed to teach me all there is to know about tobacco growing."

"Are you our servant?" I asked. "Oh, maybe I shouldn't have asked that." Shut your mouth, Katherine, I thought.

"It's all right to ask, Miss Eastwood," he said with a smile. "I'm not your servant. I paid the cost of the ocean journey myself. But now I'm out of money."

"So you're staying with us until you learn about growing tobacco. How nice."

Edward slapped at a mosquito on his cheek and said, "Yes. I'm staying here until I'm ready to start a plantation on my own fifty acres. And it is nice."

The Virginia colony would give Mr. Hollyman fifty acres of land, as they did to all gentlemen who came here. Then he would have his own place. He was here to stay. For some reason, that made me feel happy.

I fell asleep that night thinking about Father's surprise, about having my brother with us again, and about the nice Mr. Hollyman. The mosquitoes didn't even bother me.

In the morning, I sat at the riverbank and watched the men unload the ship. The day was hot and steamy.

"Robert, open your jacket," Mother instructed. "Edward, you too. It's best not to get overheated."

I saw a look of worry in her eyes. We called summer the seasoning time for newcomers. You either made it through the first summer in Virginia or you died. She was thinking of Rosemund and Henry and all the servants who didn't live.

Bundles, barrels, and trunks were being stacked up on the wharf. I knew what must be in some of them. Each year when the tobacco crop was good and we had money, Father would order supplies. Mostly, we got basic things. There would be tools that Father needed and bolts of cloth for bedding and clothes. And shoes. Sometimes, he ordered more livestock.

Suddenly, Mother started to cry. "Oh, William. You didn't."

I looked at the supplies being unloaded. There sat a load of bricks. Another load was being lowered from the ship.

Father put his arm around Mother. "I did, my dear. There are enough bricks here for two chimneys. You're going to have a fine new house."

"English bricks," she said and threw her arms around him. I ran to Mother and Father and hugged them both.

"I've never seen a lady cry over bricks before," Robert said to us as he watched.

"You don't understand what this means," I said. "Mother is happy because our times in the cottage are over." I couldn't

22

explain it to him. Mother was a lady. Although she'd never complained about the cottage, a real house meant everything to her. A real house with a brick chimney was something she dreamed about. Now she would have two chimneys. That meant two fireplaces — one for the main room and one for the sleeping room. We'd be warmer during the winter. How could Robert ever understand how hard it had been on her?

"Father," I said, " this is your best surprise ever. That's why you've been saving that pile of boards in the woods."

"You little fox," he laughed. "When were you out there? You weren't supposed to see the boards for the new house."

Robert walked over. "Here comes a surprise for you, Father." He pointed up to where a horse was held in the air by ropes and a sling. "It's a gift from Uncle. One of his riding horses."

As the horse was slowly lowered, it shrieked and twisted against the ropes. Father shook his head and kept saying, "My, my." He was really surprised. We didn't have a riding horse. In Virginia, we traveled mostly by river and had very few roads. There weren't many horses here.

"Uncle says you can't be a gentleman without a horse," Robert told Father.

"How exciting." I twirled around. "A house and a horse. Aren't we fine people now?"

Mother gave me a look. "Behave, Katherine," she said.

Robert grasped my arm and smiled. "Yes, behave, Kat. Or I won't let you have the gifts Uncle sent for you."

Surprises for me? I couldn't bear it.

IV
TERRIBLE NEWS

A beautiful new trunk from the ship sat on the floor of the cottage. Robert opened the lid and asked, "Are you ready, Kat?"

"Yes, get on with it," I said. Mother sighed at my bad manners. "Please."

"All right," Robert said as he lifted a bolt of cloth from the trunk. "Mother, this is Uncle's gift for you."

She pulled back the edge of material and gasped. It was lovely black silk. What fine gowns Anne could make from this. "How wonderful," Mother said. She held the cloth in her lap and smoothed it with her hand again and again.

Robert handed her another parcel. In it was white cloth and lace for collars and cuffs. "And this is the latest style," he said as he handed her a tall black hat. "All the ladies are wearing them."

I wriggled impatiently. Mother was too overcome to notice. Robert dug in the trunk, pretending he couldn't find what he was looking for. He was a tease.

"Robert, hurry!"

"Ah, here it is," he said finally. "Something for Kat."

I unwrapped the cloth that hid the surprise inside. "Oh," I squealed. "Oh!"

It was the loveliest gown I'd ever seen. I stood to shake it out to full length. "Look at this." The gown was green velvet with the new high waist. Ribbons sewn into the sleeves made puffs at the elbows. The hip pads in the skirt made the gown stand out at the sides. I hugged the gown to my chest.

"Mother, help me put it on. Now," I said and pulled her into the sleeping room. I ripped off my old clothes. Mother smiled. She held the gown high so I could slip into it.

"It's perfect for you, darling," she said as she laced it up. "Go show Robert."

Robert loved it too. I patted the wide skirts and put my hands on the fitted waist. Walking back and forth to show it off, I asked over and over, "Do you like it?"

"It needs shoes," Robert said and handed me another parcel. In it were two pairs of shoes. One pair was for everyday, and the other was very fancy. I quickly slipped on a pair. It was pure bliss. They actually fit.

"There's more." Robert pulled out a black wool winter cloak for me and a bolt of dark blue cloth for everyday dresses. Then he placed a tiny package in my hands.

Opening it, I saw a small framed painting of a young man. "Who's this?" I asked. The young man was not very good-looking.

"That's Dudley, the son of Mother's cousin, John Newton."

"Dudley Newton," I said. "Isn't that nice." I was puzzled. I barely remembered Cousin John's family. I couldn't really place Dudley. He might have been the oldest son of the family, but I wasn't sure. If he was that boy, I remembered not liking him when we met in England long ago. That boy had been horrible and mean.

Robert said, "That's the man you're going to . . ."

Mother interrupted. "That's enough, Robert. Katherine has had enough surprises for one day." She took the painting away from me.

Robert nodded. "Sorry, Mother."

"What's this all about?" I asked. I was suddenly frightened, and I didn't know why.

"Not now, Katherine." Mother folded up the wrapping cloth

and put the gifts back into the trunk.

That made me angry. I was being treated like a child. I raised my voice. "Tell me, Mother." She wouldn't even look at me. Robert pushed the trunk against the wall and didn't say a word.

Just then, Father came into the cottage. He pretended to be confused. "Who's the pretty lass in the green dress?" he asked. Then he felt the tension in the room. "What's wrong here?"

I couldn't hold it in any longer. In a burst of temper, I told him, "I got a painting of that awful Dudley Newton. And Mother and Robert won't tell me why. It's not fair." I started to cry. I had a terrible inkling of what this was all about.

"Poor Katherine," Father said as he put his arm around me. "You're right. It's not fair to keep a secret from you."

Mother didn't agree and said so. "Really, William. It's not the right time to talk about it."

"Please, Father," I said through my tears. I almost didn't want to know, but I looked up at him and begged him to tell me.

"I can't refuse you when you look like a wet chicken," he said, pushing the hair from my face and wiping my tears.

"Your mother and I have arranged for you to marry Dudley Newton. He is Cousin John's heir and will someday own the Newton land." Father's eyes were a little misty. "It's a very good marriage for you. You'll be sent home to England soon. After some years, the marriage will take place."

I put my hands over my ears and screamed, "No!" I wouldn't listen to this. It couldn't be true. I jerked away from Father and ran from the cottage and out of the palisade.

When I heard Father calling me, I didn't turn back. Instead, I picked up the skirts of the beautiful green velvet gown and ran faster into the woods. It was a long time before I stopped running. And even longer before I stopped crying.

They can't do this to me, I thought. I sat on a tree stump and wiped away my tears.

Father said they'd send me home to England. How silly. England wasn't my home. Didn't he know that? Virginia was my home. Being here with my family was home to me. I had no desire to return to stupid old England.

What about marriage? Well, I wasn't shocked that my parents had thought about my getting married. Every girl dreams of getting married someday, and I knew the time was coming for me. I'd be the right age in not too many more years. But Dudley Newton? Ugh! What a terrible thought. I didn't want to marry Dudley. How could they do this to me?

I took a deep breath. I made myself feel strong and determined. Well, I thought, I won't do it. I'll refuse. I won't marry Dudley Newton. I won't leave Virginia. If they insist, I'll think of some way to get out of it. I will.

"Miss Eastwood, are you all right?" Edward Hollyman startled me as he approached.

"Yes, thank you," I said. As he helped me to my feet, I noticed his kind blue eyes again. "Virginia is a wonderful place, Mr. Hollyman. You're very lucky to be here." I couldn't stop talking. "You'll have a good life in Virginia. It will be hard work, but you'll make it. You can raise your family here." What was I talking about? I blushed and said quickly, "Virginia is a good place to make your home."

Edward said, "I couldn't agree with you more." Then he shot the musket he was carrying into the air and shouted, "Robert, over here. I've found her."

Robert rode through the woods on the new riding horse from Uncle. He was like a knight come to save me. Edward gave me a boost up onto the horse behind my brother, and I put my arms around his waist. The horse carried us away.

"Are you better, Kat?" Robert asked, turning to look at me. I leaned against his back and gave him a hug.

"I'm very well, thank you."

"I wouldn't have thought so," Robert laughed. "You ran out of the cottage like a wild Indian."

"But now I'm better, Robert."

"Why?"

"Because I'm not going to marry Dudley Newton," I said with determination. "That's why."

"Uh-oh."

I poked my finger at his back. "And I'm not going to leave Virginia. What do you think of that?"

"I think you'll be put on the ship whether you like it or not," Robert said.

"Then when I reach England, I'll hire on as a servant and come right back. Wouldn't that surprise everyone?" I asked. "Really, Robert, I don't want to go. This is my home. You don't understand what it means to me."

That made him angry. "Oh, yes I do, Kat. I certainly do. Not that it will make any difference to Mother and Father."

He was very upset. He's thinking about his own life, I thought suddenly. Robert's home was England, and he was here whether he liked it or not. Maybe he didn't like Virginia at all. Maybe he was unhappy here. I hadn't even thought about it. Had Robert asked to stay in England? Did Father make him come to Virginia anyway? Oh dear. Would Father make me go to England?

We rode through the woods in silence. I didn't feel quite as brave anymore.

The ship left that same day. Robert and I sat on the horse, watching as the ship turned around slowly and headed downriver. Robert waved and stared after it until it disappeared from view. He was silent. He's sad, I thought, and I'm afraid. What a terrible day.

Then Robert turned the horse, and we went up the path to the palisade.

V
SEASONING TIME

It took a few days for things to settle down again. Mother and Father said I'd come to like the idea of going to England and marrying Dudley. I disagreed firmly. It didn't help. They said that I must do it anyway. But for now we'd say no more about the matter. There was plenty of time to get used to the idea, they told me. Never, I thought.

Edward moved into the barn with the men. He worked all day in the tobacco fields with Father and the others. Robert rode the horse to get it into shape after its long trip. Mother and Anne were busy sorting out shoes and cloth. They planned clothes for the servants and new gowns for Mother and me.

On Sunday, after returning from church in Jamestown, we planned the new house. Father drew up the plans as Mother, Robert, Edward, and I gave him ideas.

"There's wood enough for two stories," Father said. "You shall have wood floors too, Elizabeth, instead of dirt."

Mother was beaming. I knew how tired she was of our dirt floor.

"We'll have two outside chimneys made out of our English bricks," said Father as he showed us the outline of the house. "We'll put a chimney at each end. There could be two big rooms downstairs, each one with its own fireplace."

Mother had an idea. "If we had the front and back doors open into the same room, it might help in summer. With the doors open, the breezes would blow right through." She sketched her idea on the plan with her finger. "It would be cool and lovely."

"Splendid," Father agreed. "We'll have our main room and the sleeping room downstairs. Upstairs will be real sleeping rooms too. No more loft for you, Katherine."

If you don't send me to England, I thought.

"Where are we going to build the house?" Robert asked.

"It will remain inside the palisade," Father answered, "for protection against Indian attack."

"If I may offer an idea," Edward said. "A good place for the house is at back of the palisade. It would be rather close to the fence, but the view from there is best. Then next year you could move back the fence. You know, enlarge the area."

"Thank you, Edward," said Mother. "That's an excellent idea. Could we do that, William?"

Father said we could. Everyone was excited about the house. Work would begin at once. Father's carpenter and the new men would build it.

Early the next morning, I watched as the men paced out the shape of the house and marked the post holes. The oxen and cart were taken into the woods to bring back Father's hidden pile of boards. Robert rode off to explore our land, and I left the palisade to find something to do.

I saw the new servants, Alice and Mercey, feeding the chickens and ducks behind the women's house. Good, I thought. There was nothing I liked more than talking to newcomers. It gave me a chance to share what I knew about the plantation and to learn about them.

"I'm from London, Miss," Alice said when I asked about her home. Her parents had died, so she signed on to come to Virginia. "In London there was nothing for me. No work and no food. People said there were husbands to be had in Virginia. So I came."

There was a very good chance for Alice to be married here. Since there were far fewer women in Virginia than men, I had no

doubt that she'd find a husband. That is, if she lived that long. I was worried about Alice, who was very thin.

"Where did you come from, Mercey?" I asked the other girl. She looked at the ground. "Farm, Miss," she mumbled. Mercey was very shy with me, but I liked her.

"Why did you come to Virginia?" I asked. If Mother had been listening, she would have said I was too nosy.

"Too many children," she said. I understood. Many of our servants came because their families couldn't feed all the children. Mercy was looking pale and sweaty in the sticky heat. Suddenly, she swayed back and forth under the hot sun. I hoped she would make it through the seasoning time.

"You must take it easy for a few days," I told them. "Eat well and go to sleep early."

Jane poked her head out the door of the women's house and said, "Miss Katherine, come here, please."

I went inside. As soon as I saw the look on her face, I knew the news was bad. "That new man is sick," Jane said.

I knew who she meant. It was the man who slept through the feast the day the ship arrived. "Just sick or bad sick?"

"Bad, I'm afraid," Jane told me.

We went to the barn to see him. Jane was right. The man was in very bad shape with the summer fever. This was how it started. Some of the servants fell ill just off the ship. For some, it took a while before the heat and mosquitoes got to them. This man might die. I had seen it happen before.

When Mother heard the news, there was fear in her eyes. It reminded her of the summer when two of her children died. She took charge quickly. She asked Sarah to brew a special tea, and we took it down to the barn.

After the man drank the tea, Mother stood outside. She fanned herself to get relief from the heat and said, "He's going to die, the poor man. Is he the only one who's sick?"

"As far as I know," I answered her.

"Well, we must thank God for that," she said, looking up at the sky. "Pray for rain, dear, to cool things down."

That morning, I prayed for rain. Later in the day, I began to pray for my brother. It was noon when Edward carried Robert into the cottage. He had fainted and fallen from the horse. It was the summer fever. Mother's worst fears had come true.

She put Robert into her bed and stayed at the cottage to be at his side. I took over her other duties, including nursing the sick. In the days that followed, more servants fell ill — both newcomers and some of the others. It was the worst sickness in three years. I spent most of each day at the barn and the women's house. The man died first, then Alice. Mercey was sick. Robert lay in the bed lost in fever.

The tobacco couldn't be ignored, and Father kept the work going in the fields. The new house began to take shape. Mother winced at each blow of the hammer. She wanted Robert alive. The house didn't mean anything to her now.

One day when I returned to the cottage, Mother whispered to me, "Robert has been asking for you. Sit with him for a while."

"Of course, Mother."

She squeezed my arm tightly and said, "Behave yourself. Don't tire or upset him." She didn't have to tell me that.

I sat on a stool next to the bed. Finally, Robert opened his eyes and found me there.

"Dear Kat," he said weakly. "I hate Virginia."

I put a cold, wet cloth on his forehead. His eyes closed again, and he sighed. After a few minutes, he asked, "Are you still here, Kat?"

"I'm here," I said and took his hand.

"Don't you ever fix your hair?" Robert asked, turning his head and looking at me. "You look terrible."

"Not as bad as you do." It slipped out before I could think.

He smiled. "I can't laugh. I'm too weak."

"I know. I'm sorry."

We didn't speak for several minutes. I thought Robert was sleeping again. I was so frightened for him. My tears dripped down on the thin hand I held in my own.

"Don't cry. I'm not dead yet." He wasn't sleeping.

"Don't say it," I begged.

"You know, Kat, I would rather die than stay in Virginia."

"Please, Robert."

"England is . . ." He shivered and tossed his head from side to side. "England is my home."

Finally, when Robert fell into a deep sleep, I left the cottage. It started to rain. The walls of the new house were up, and the two chimneys were almost completed. My house, I thought, as the rain beat down on me. My home.

Wasn't life strange? I wanted to stay in Virginia and was told to go to England. Robert wanted to stay in England and was made to come to Virginia. How mixed up it all was. We couldn't even trade places. Father wanted his son to be here with him, I guessed. And he wanted his daughter to have a good marriage in England.

Robert couldn't have meant that he'd rather die than stay here. He was giving up. I kicked at the ground and stomped my feet in a puddle. Well, I wasn't going to give up. Virginia was my home. I wouldn't leave. I wouldn't. I was going to fight. I'd make Robert fight too.

I went back into the cottage to Robert and squeezed his hand hard. "You're not going to die, Brother," I hissed in his ear.

VI
THE LETTER

"You're going to live," I told Robert over and over again. I visited him whenever I could and whispered it in his ear. Sometimes he was asleep. When he was awake, he'd tell me to go away and stop being such a bother.

I wanted Mercey to live too. Poor Alice had died very quickly. Now Mercey had been ill for many days. I thought that she might get better if she was reminded of the farm in England. I brought a little duckling into the women's house and placed it on her bedding. It stayed at her side. It thought she was its mother. Each day I'd make Mercey drink the special tea and tell her that she was going to live. The duckling needed her.

Little by little, Mercey got better. One day when I came to see her, I found her sitting up and holding the duckling.

"Does it have a name?" I asked.

Mercey smiled at me. "Sam, Miss. After my brother."

"What a good name," I said. "Jane, Sam shall be Mercey's duck. You must be sure that we don't have him for dinner." I turned to Mercey. "We'll tie a cloth around his neck so Jane won't forget which duck is Sam."

"Thank you, Miss," Mercey said as she petted Sam's feathers. Then she looked up at me. "I'm better now. I'll be able to work soon. I know all about growing things."

"I'm so happy. I need a good friend like you," I said and meant it. She reminded me of Rosemund.

Our new house was finished, and we moved our things into the rooms. Father carried Robert across the yard to the house. It seemed to make Robert get better, being there. He slowly improved until the day came when Mother smiled again. He was going to live.

Mother sang as she arranged our things in the new house. She loved the sound of her shoes on the wood floors. Sarah was proud of the brick fireplace where she cooked and said the food would be better than ever.

Robert became well enough to sit in the main room and visit. Mother was right. With both doors open, the breezes blew through and made it very pleasant.

Life was brighter, but it wasn't exactly a happy time for Robert and me. Although I tried not to think about the future, the matter of Dudley Newton was looming over me. Robert, I guessed, was trying to be brave about living in Virginia for the rest of his life. We couldn't figure out what to do about it.

Then suddenly, everything changed.

Father returned from Jamestown one day and announced that he'd gotten a letter from Uncle. He took Mother and Robert into the other room for a private talk. When they came out, Robert's face was glowing. Father and Mother looked serious. It must be important news, I thought.

"Take a walk with me, Katherine," Father said. He took my arm as we left the house.

"Uncle sent us some news, my girl," he said. "His only son, Thomas, has died. He's made Robert his heir. When Uncle dies, Robert will own the land in England."

"I understand," I said.

"Uncle wants Robert to return to England now," Father said.

I let out a wild shriek. "How wonderful, Father. That's just what Robert wants. It'll make him so happy."

"You surprise me, Katherine. I thought you'd be very upset to hear the news of his going."

I shook my head. "No, Father. I'm glad that Robert is going to have what he wants most of all. He was very unhappy about leaving England."

"He was?" Father asked.

"Yes, it's true," I said. "He's not like us. We're Virginians now, and this is our home. Robert's home is England."

Father fell silent. We walked on.

Finally, he spoke. "I noticed the work you did during the sickness. You took over all your mother's duties. It was an excellent job, Katherine."

I looked up at him.

"What do you know about working with tobacco?" he asked.

It was time to be honest. "Everything," I said.

"And growing the food crops?"

"Everything."

"Tending the livestock?"

"That too," I said, getting worried about where this talk was leading. I wasn't supposed to know these things. Now that I was found out, was I going to be punished?

"Cooking?" he asked.

"No, but only because Mother was close by. She told me it was no job for a lady."

He laughed. "So she would." Then he grew serious again. "She's been trying to prepare you for a life in England as the wife of a wealthy man."

I kicked at a clod of dirt and said, "Oh, bother."

Father got a twinkle in his eye. "I don't think you'd do very well in England, Katherine. You're not a lady at all. You're a wild thing."

"I am," I said, waiting for what was coming next.

"But you're perfect for Virginia." He put his hands on my shoulders and smiled at me. "We'll have to keep you here."

"I can stay?" I asked, hardly believing what I heard.

"Yes," Father laughed. "We must keep one young Eastwood in Virginia. We'll write a letter to your mother's Cousin John and . . ."

41

"And tell Dudley to find another wife!" I doubled over with giggles. "Stupid old England and stupid old Dudley Newton. I'm staying in Virginia." I danced a jig on that very spot.

Robert was so happy for me. Mother was too. She said that it would have broken her heart to lose me. She had only wanted what was best for me, and to her that meant an easy life in England. I think she had begun to understand that I was a tough Virginia girl now.

We turned our attention to getting Robert back to full strength. It took time. But by early autumn, he was healthy once again and ready to return to England. We had a feast in his honor before he left. It gave me a chance to wear my green gown.

"You look like a queen," Robert teased me. I was carrying a jug of cider from the house.

"You go too far," I said. "Don't you think so, Mr. Hollyman?" I was looking for more compliments.

Edward said, "Let me think about that."

Robert laughed. "I'm not the only tease in the world, Kat."

I pulled at Robert's ear and said, "At least I won't have to put up with you much longer."

"But you'll have to put up with Edward. I'm teaching him how to tease you and make you angry," Robert said.

"Then you're going to stay in Virginia?" I asked Edward. Robert had offered him a position on Uncle's estate in England. I didn't know what Edward had decided.

"Yes, I am," Edward said. "Robert isn't too happy about that. I'm not sure he believes me when I tell him how much I like Virginia." He smiled at me. "I have reasons to stay."

"Well, I find it hard to believe," said Robert stubbornly.

I don't, I thought.

We said our good-byes to Robert the next day. Just before he boarded the ship that would take him away, I gave him a tiny wrapped package.

As the ship pulled away from the wharf, I shouted to him to open the package. It was the painting of Dudley Newton.

"Give it back to him," I shouted. "And tell him . . ."

"Tell him to find another wife?" Robert yelled back.

"Yes. And tell him I'm sorry. But not very much."

Robert waved from the ship. Mother, Father, Edward, and I waved from the shore. I heard Robert calling, "I love you all."

* * *

I still remember that last time I saw Robert. He is doing well in England and writes often to tell me what is happening to him and his new family. He's married now. He wrote a letter about the birth of his daughter. She has red hair like yours, he wrote, so we named her Katherine.

So there's a Katherine Eastwood in England after all. I'm so thankful it's not me. I'm here in my beloved Virginia where I belong. Father says he would have had to tie me up and throw me on the ship to get me to leave. What a wild thing. He shakes his head when he remembers.

Our plantation is thriving. The new house has proven to be cool in summer and warm in winter. I made Father name it Two Chimneys. Mother likes that, because houses in England have names. Houses in Virginia should have names too. When people talk about our place, they no longer call it Eastwood's Plantation. We're going to visit Two Chimneys, they say.

Today many people are arriving at Two Chimneys. There are boats tying up all along the riverbank. It's my wedding day. Edward and I are getting married.

We're going to stay here at Two Chimneys. Someday this place and Edward's land will belong to our children, who will be the first in the family born here. I want a son named Henry and a daughter named Rosemund. And Edward thinks we ought to have one more son to name after Robert, his good friend who brought him to Virginia.

AMERICA'S
PAST

The Trip to Jamestown

In 1606, no English people lived in North America. They had tried to start a colony twenty years earlier. This was on Roanoke Island off the coast of what is now North Carolina. The colonists didn't survive. No one knows what happened to them.

This map shows the route taken by the next group of colonists who left England for the new land.

FIRST ENGLISH COLONY

In December of 1606, three ships left England — the Susan Constant, *the* Godspeed, *and the* Discovery. *The ships carried 105 adventurers and their supplies of tools, weapons, and food. The gentlemen, craftsmen, and workers were going to start a colony in the New World.*

The ships were expected to reach the West Indies in four weeks. But bad weather kept them close to England for six weeks before they could move on. First, they sailed south. They stopped at the Canary Islands and took on fresh water.

Then the ships began the dangerous journey across the Atlantic Ocean to the West Indies. Life on the ships was crowded and unhealthy. Some of the passengers were ill. It was not until March of 1607 that they reached the island of Martinique in the West Indies. There the colonists rested for three weeks.

They sailed from island to island. Finally, they left the islands

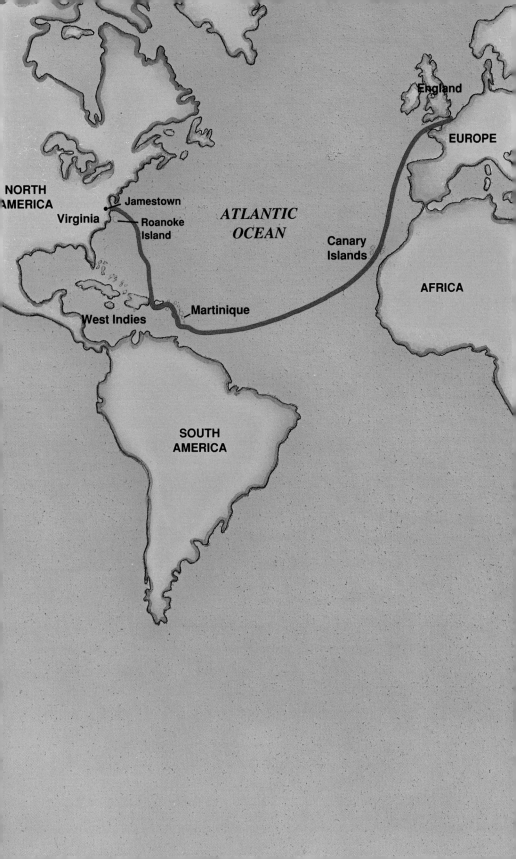

Inside the fort, the Jamestown settlers built their homes.

and sailed north. They ran into a violent storm. The captain of the Discovery *wanted to go back to England when he couldn't find land. But all three ships kept going. In late April, they spotted the coast of Virginia.*

They saw a beautiful land full of trees and wildlife. Indians could be seen on shore. The first task was to pick a site for their settlement. Men who were assigned to explore the area told of a great river going many miles inland. The ships sailed up the river, which they named the James River after King James of England.

In May, the colonists found the place they had been looking for. It was a three-mile-long strip of land running parallel to the riverbank, almost an island. Only a narrow piece of land connected it to the mainland. With water nearly all around, this place would be easy to defend. Also, the water was deep, and the ships could be tied to the trees right there.

The Susan Constant *was one of three ships that arrived in Virginia in 1607.*

The colonists began to build a fort, crude houses, and a church. They named their new home Jamestown.